Should I Share My Ice Cream?

To Diane Camp
for always sharing her enthusiasm

ISBN 978-1-338-34358-8

12 11 10   21 22 23

Printed in the U.S.A.   40

First Scholastic printing, September 2018

This book is set in Century/Monotype; Grilled Cheese/Fontbros; Typography of Coop, Neutraface/House Industries.

Should I Share My Ice Cream?

By **Mo Willems**

An **ELEPHANT & PIGGIE** Book

SCHOLASTIC INC.

Ice cream!
Get your cold
ice cream
for a hot day!

3

Should
I share my
awesome,
yummy,
sweet,
super,
great,
tasty,
nice,
cool
ice
cream?

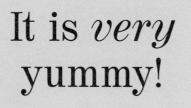

It is *very* yummy!

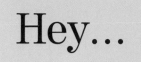

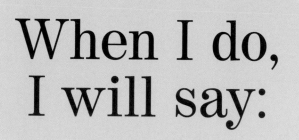

32

34

41

43

You look sad.
Would you like some
of my ice cream?

Oh, well…

Have you read all of Elephant and Piggie's funny adventures?